D0538740

Zak's LUNCH

by **Margie Palatini**   Illustrated by **Howard Fine**

Clarion Books/New York

Clarion Books
a Houghton Mifflin Company imprint
215 Park Avenue South, New York, NY 10003
Text copyright © 1998 by Margie Palatini
Illustrations copyright © 1998 by Howard Fine

The text type is set in 16/24-point Caslon.
The illustrations for this book were executed in watercolor and pastel.

Printed in the USA.

Library of Congress Cataloging-in-Publication Data

Palatini, Margie.
Zak's lunch / by Margie Palatini ; illustrated by Howard Fine.
p.   cm.
Summary: Rather than eat his boring old ham and cheese sandwich, Zak conjures up Lou,
a waitress who serves him a delectable feast for the imagination.
ISBN 0-395-81674-2
[1. Food–Fiction. 2. Dinners and Dining–Fiction.] I. Fine, Howard, ill. II. Title.

PZ7.P1755Zak   1998
[E]–dc21   97-18799
CIP
AC

HOR 10 9 8 7 6 5 4 3 2 1

For Michael and Molly
WOOF!
–M.P.

For my parents
–H.F.

4

"Lunchtime," called Mother.

Zak skipped down the stairs two at a time and ran into the kitchen. George pounded close behind and skidded across the linoleum.

Zak stopped. George stopped.

"Yechhh!" said Zak.

"Yechhh what?" said Mother.

"Yechhh *that*," said Zak, pointing to his plate and making a yucky face. "Ham and cheese."

"WOOF," said George.

"I don't want any old ham and cheese sandwich for lunch!
It's . . . it's . . . too hammy. Too cheesy. And who wants mustard breath?"
Zak folded his arms in front of his chest. "I won't eat it. And that's that."
"That's that?" said Mother.
"That's that," said Zak.
"This is not a restaurant, young man," said Mother. "Now, no more
of your excuses, and none of your tricks. I want that lunch *gone*.
And *that's* that."

Jeesh. Mother was having an ornery day, thought Zak. A very
ornery day. But Zak was having a pretty ornery day himself.

He stared at the sandwich and mumbled. "Zgxgrr*mbbl!" And
he grumbled. "Xxmsl!o*grbms!" And then he grumbled some more.
"This is not a restaurant. Hmmf! Well, it should be a restaurant.
My very own restaurant where I could eat anything I wanted.
As much as I wanted. Anytime I wanted. And it wouldn't be
any ol' hammy ham sandwich with cheese that's all full of holes.
And *that's* that. Right, George?"

"WOOF."

"What's what, kiddo?"

Zak looked up.

Smiling at him with a big toothy grin was a waitress with frizzy red curls and a teeny tiny frilly hat that sat right on top of her head. She wore a pale blue uniform with a big pocket. Written above the pocket in thick red thread was the name *Lou.*

Zak looked at Lou.

Lou looked at Zak.

Zak looked around the room. It didn't look like his kitchen. It didn't smell like his kitchen.

And there was no ham and cheese sandwich in sight. What was in sight was a big sign in bright purple neon lights that said ZAK'S PLACE.

Lou pulled a pencil from behind her ear, wet the tip with her tongue, and tapped her order pad.

"Ready and waitin'. Let her rip!"

"Really?" said Zak.

Lou laughed. "Do rolls roll? Do beets beat? Does chili chill?"

Zak grinned. "I'll have a hamburger."

"A hamburger!" Lou wailed. "Isn't that just an eensy teensy bit *boring*?"

"A *double* cheeseburger, maybe?" said Zak with a tad of hesitation.

Lou sighed and nodded to the sign that said ZAK'S PLACE.

"Work with me, cupcake. Work with me."

Zak looked at the sign.

He looked at Lou.

Zak looked at George.

George looked at Zak.

"Okay then. Here goes," Zak said, taking a deep breath.

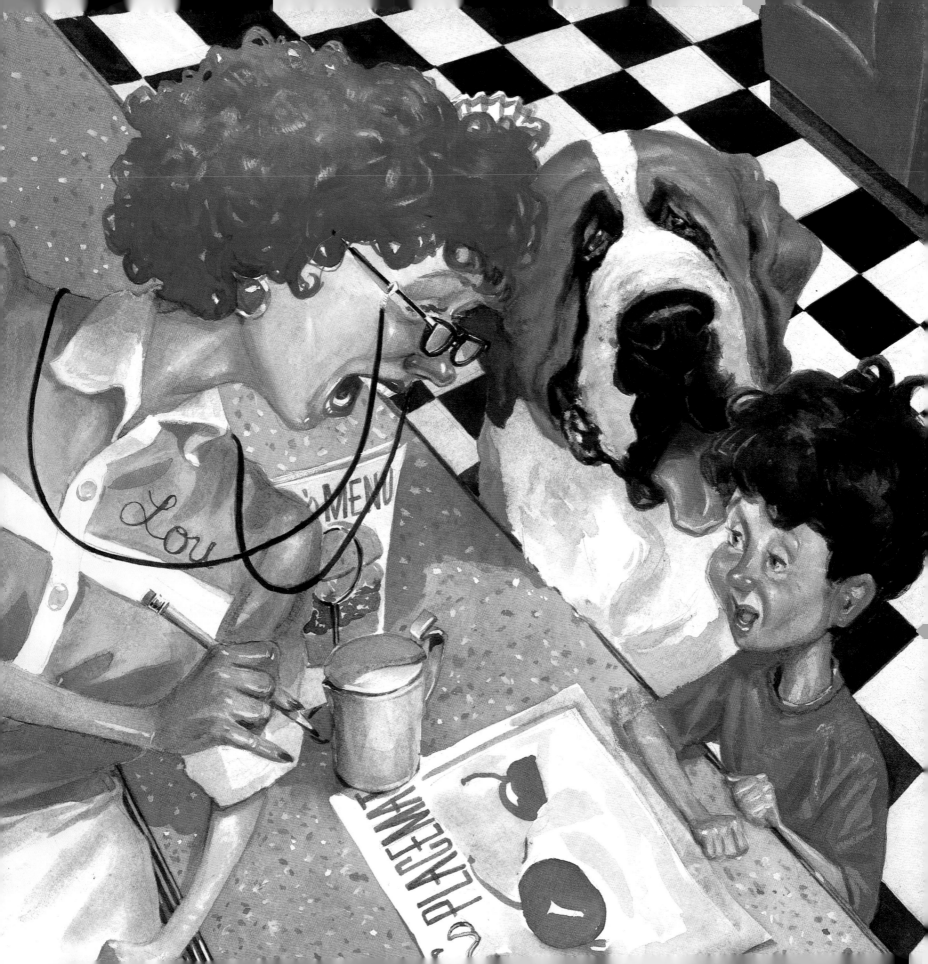

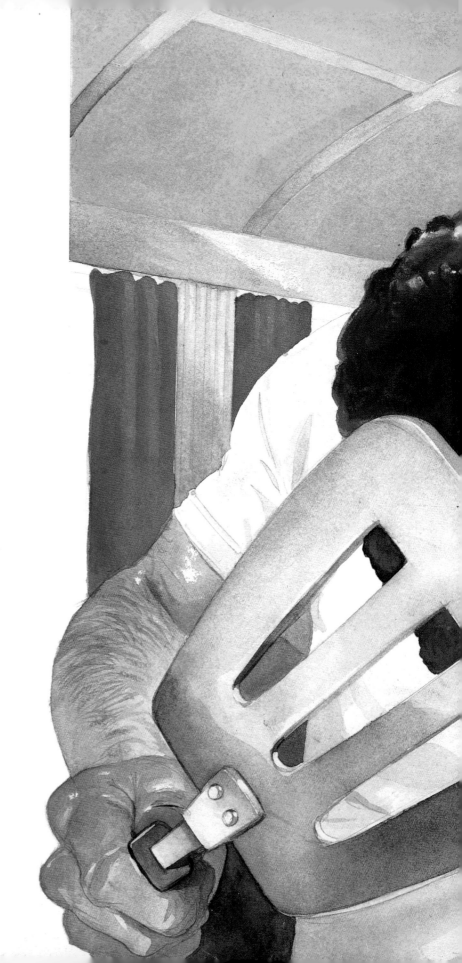

"Make that a triple-decker, super-duper burger deluxe. With *lots* of grease, and runny ketchup, fried onions, gooey yellow cheese that squirts at you when you take a bite, and at least a pound of pickles. The kind that make your mouth pucker."

"Now we're talkin'!" Lou said, scribbling the order on her pad.

"Hey, Cookie," she called out. "One moo meat all the way. And don't be cheap with the grease!"

Zak looked down the long pink counter and watched a man in an apron and a paper hat flip hamburgers while the griddle crackled and spat. Zak smiled a satisfactory Zak smile and gave himself a spin on the stool.

"What else?" asked Lou.

"Hmmm . . . french fries," ordered Zak thoughtfully. "Lots and lots of french fries. Pile them this high," he said, putting his left hand way above the top of his head. "Skinnies and ziggies and the kind that curlicue around and around. And a pizza!"

He looked at George.

"Make that two, Lou. Big ones. Like this." Zak stretched his arms wide. "With sausage. Pepperoni. Onions, peppers, mushrooms, extra cheese. The works, Lou. The works!"

"WOOF." George approved.

Cookie really cooked fast food fast.

Before Zak blinked, there was his triple-decker, super-duper cheeseburger deluxe, a pile of skinny, ziggy, and curlicue fries, and two pizzas as big as bicycle tires, right in front of him.

Gooey yellow cheese squirted clear across the room as Zak took a bite of burger.

"Perfect, Lou! Perfect!"

"What else, dumplin'?" asked Lou, cracking her gum.

Zak wiped pickle juice from his chin as George slurped the cheese off the top of his pizza.

"Got any chicken?" asked Zak with a pickle pucker.

Lou nodded.

"Make it all drumsticks."

17

"Fry the bird. All pins,"
Lou called out to Cookie.

Zak stuffed a handful of ziggies into his mouth, picked a piece of pepperoni off one of the slices of pizza, and tossed it to George.

"And we'll both have a tub of spaghetti with meatballs the size of baseballs. And some hot dogs, please. With chili. And nachos with cheese. And onion rings. Don't forget the onion rings. George loves onion rings. Right, boy?"

"WOOF."

19

Lou nodded and scribbled.

Scribbled and nodded.

And Cookie cooked and cooked.

"Working up a thirst yet, cupcake?" asked Lou as Zak sucked up a long strand of spaghetti.

Zak cleared an opening on the counter and peeked through the mountain of meatballs.

"What do you have to drink?"

"Everything," said Lou.

"Line 'em up," ordered Zak.

21

Colas, root beers, orange pops, lemonades, cherry fizzes, frosties, slushes, ice cream sodas of every flavor heaped with whipped cream and topped with cherries, and chocolate shakes so thick the straws stood straight up in the glasses squeezed their way onto the table.

Zak sipped, slurped, and chugalugged a taste from each and every one until he thought his belly would burst.

"So, what else can I get you, kiddo?" asked Lou as Zak polished off a second triple root beer float.

Zak burped. George belched.

Then they both licked some chili off Zak's fingers and thought.

"Hey!" cried Lou. "I know just what you're craving."

"You do?" said Zak.

"Lou do," said Lou. "Dessert. Comin' at ya!"

Before Zak and George had time for another burp or belch, pies began sliding down the counter. Pie after pie after pie after pie after pie. Cherries and berries. Creams and meringues.

Then came cookies. And brownies. Candies and fudge.

Zak had only tasted one berry and a slurp of meringue before Lou wheeled in a three-tiered chocolate cake almost as tall as she was. It was covered with goops and gobs of pink icing and drips and drops of chocolate syrup. It even had colored candy sprinkles stuck all over the sides and top.

"Go to it!" said Lou, handing Zak a fork.

George and Zak were tunneling their way through the bottom layer with banana filling when Lou started trucking in the ice cream. She put her fingers between her teeth and gave a whistle.

Lights lit. Beeps beeped. And then, *schlurp! schlosh! schlump!* The load of ice cream landed. Vanilla here. Chocolate there. Strawberry and cookie-crumble-surprise everywhere in between.

"Yoo-hoo!" echoed a voice from the other side of the mountain of vanilla.

"Lou? Is that you?" Zak called back, sliding belly first down a hill of chocolate.

"Yoo-hoo!"

"Lou?"

"Zak?"

"Lou?"

"Zak?"

"Lou?"

"*Who?*"

"Huh?"

"WOOF!"

"Zak? *Who* are you talking to?" said Mother.

Zak looked around the room.

There was no mountain of vanilla.

No hill of chocolate.

There wasn't even a melted puddle of strawberry
or one single crumb of cookie-crumble-surprise.

No Lou. No Cookie.

No sign that said ZAK'S PLACE.

There was only George. And Zak. And Mother.

And . . . Zak's lunch.

"Zak, I told you. I want to see that sandwich *gone*."

Zak grumbled. He groaned. He made a yucky face.
There it was. That ol' ham and cheese sandwich
still staring him right in the face. Why, anybody
could see it was much too, *much* too hammy.
Too, too, too, too cheesy.
And no way,
no how,
did he want mustard breath!

Zak looked at George.
George looked at Zak.
George looked at Zak's lunch.
And his nose got closer . . .
and closer . . . and . . .
When Zak looked thisaway,
his lunch just went . . .
thataway.
"Well now, you see there, Zak,"
Mother said. "I knew you could
make that lunch disappear.
Good boy."